FAMOUS TALES

Puss in Boots

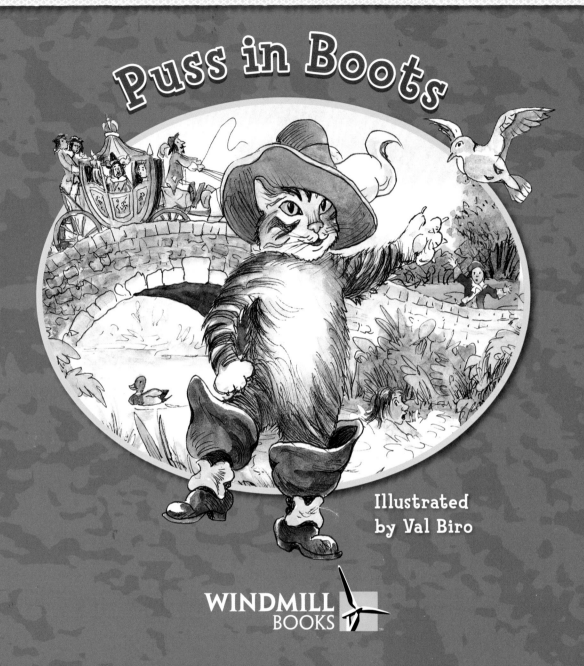

Illustrated
by Val Biro

WINDMILL
BOOKS

Published in 2017 by **Windmill Books**, an Imprint of Rosen Publishing. 29 East 21st Street, New York, NY 10010

Copyright © 2017 Award Publications

Cataloging-in-Publication Data
Names: Biro, Val, illustrator.
Title: Puss in boots / illustrated by Val Biro.
Description: New York : Windmill Books, 2016. | Series: Famous tales.
Identifiers: ISBN 9781499480672 (pbk.) | ISBN 9781499480610 (library bound) | ISBN 9781499480498 (6 pack)
Subjects: LCSH: Puss in Boots (Tale)--Juvenile fiction. | Cats--Juvenile fiction. | Kings and rulers--Juvenile fiction.
Classification: LCC PZ7.B5233 Pu 2016 | DDC [F]--dc23

Manufactured in the United States of America
CPSIA Compliance Information: Batch #BS16PK: For Further Information contact Rosen Publishing, New York, New York at 1-800-237-9932.

Once upon a time, there lived a miller and his three sons. When the miller died he left the mill to his eldest son, his donkey to the middle son, and his cat to the youngest son.

The youngest son was of course unhappy
with this. Until the cat spoke to him!

"Do not worry, young master.
Fetch me some boots and a sack.
Everything will be alright."

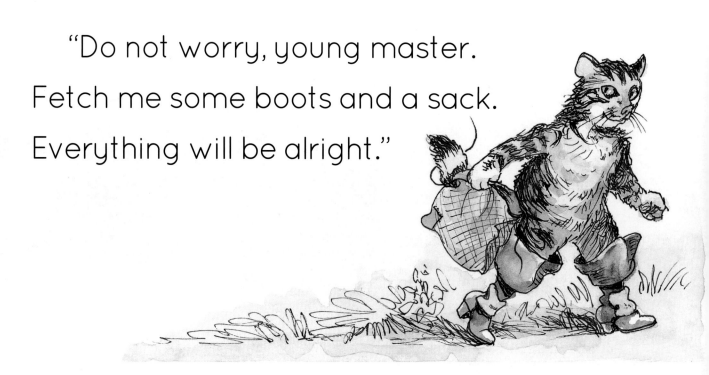

The youngest son did as the cat asked.
Puss went off to the forest and captured
a rabbit in the sack.

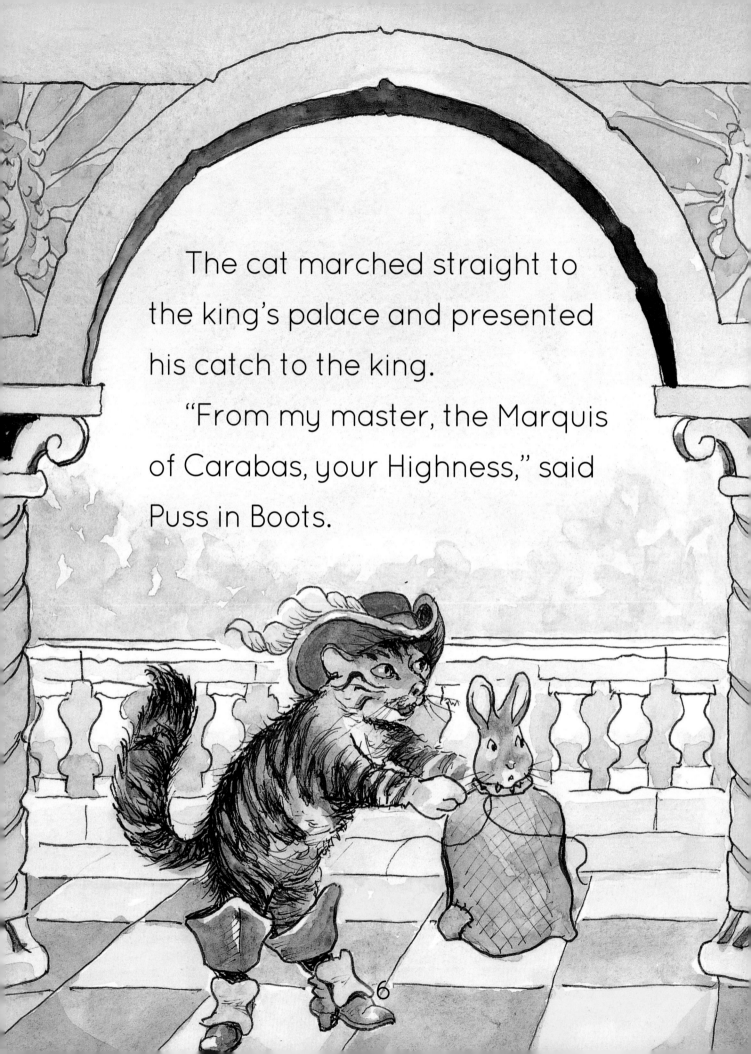

The cat marched straight to the king's palace and presented his catch to the king.

"From my master, the Marquis of Carabas, your Highness," said Puss in Boots.

6

"Thank your master,"
replied the king.

7

The next day, when Puss saw
the royal coach, he told his master
to undress and jump into
the river.

Puss hid his
master's clothes, then
cried, "Help! The Marquis of
Carabas is drowning."

9

The king recognized the name and ordered his guards to help at once.

Puss thanked the king and said, "Your majesty, while my master was bathing some robbers came and stole his clothes."

10

So the king told his servants to dress
the miller's son in the finest clothes.

When the king's daughter
saw Puss's master she fell
in love with him.

12

Then the king invited him
to ride with the princess in
the royal coach.

Puss ran ahead of the royal
coach to speak to the farmers
in a large, luscious cattle field.

"When the king asks who owns this field, tell him it is the Marquis of Carabas."

The farmers agreed happily.

Next, Puss ran ahead
to the castle of the giant.

The giant owned all the fields. But he was a tyrant and no one liked him.

"I am told you can change into anything you want." Puss asked the giant to show him.

Immediately the giant
turned into an enormous lion.

19

"That's nothing special," said Puss with a twinkle in his eye. "You're a giant. I'll be impressed if you can turn into something small... like a mouse."

The giant was vain, and liked to show off. But the moment he transformed into a mouse, Puss pounced...and ate him up!

When the royal party arrived at the
castle, Puss greeted them. "Welcome to the
castle of the Marquis of Carabas."

The king was so impressed by the Marquis of Carabas, he offered the miller's son the princess's hand in marriage.

The miller's son and the princess lived happily ever after, of course. With no small thanks to that clever cat, Puss in Boots, who lived alongside the miller's son in the castle, and was treated like a prince from that day on.